George K. Camp

Shadows

George K. Camp

Shadows

ISBN/EAN: 9783743464933

Manufactured in Europe, USA, Canada, Australia, Japa

Cover: Foto ©Andreas Hilbeck / pixelio.de

Manufactured and distributed by brebook publishing software (www.brebook.com)

George K. Camp

Shadows

SHADOWS.

BY

GEORGE K. CAMP.

SAN FRANCISCO:
A. L. BANCROFT & COMPANY.
1885.

CONTENTS.

FIXED SHADOWS.

v

CONTENTS.

SHIFTING SHADOWS.

SHADOWS OF DAWN.

FIXED SHADOWS.

THE REASON WHY.

THE reason why, I cannot tell,
　　Yet bird, and breeze, and brook, and shell,
　The same sweet song sing night and day,
　And love is woven in the lay,
Like perfume in a blossom's bell.

I feel my heart expand and swell
With sweets from out some fairy dell,
　　But naught confides, seek as I may
　　　　　　The reason why.

There is a maid whose eyes—ah, well!
They light her red lips' hydromel,
　　As star beams over roses stray—
　　Perhaps—though mind! I do not say—
Perhaps this gentle maid might tell
　　　　　　The reason why.

11

IN THE SNOW-FLAKES.

IN the snow-flakes—in the wheeling
Coronation stands she, stealing
Sly and saucy looks at me,
Looks whose half I only see
'Neath her white lids' swift revealing.

Still I catch a deeper feeling
(Which the lashes fail concealing),
Goldening futurity,
In the snow-flakes.

So I put aside appealing
To her love in this congealing
Atmosphere, and ask if we
Must forever parted be?
And there is a love's annealing
In the snow-flakes.

SHE SMILES ON ME.

SHE smiles on me, but in her downcast eyes
    That look a lullaby of silent sighs
    The silken, soft, and drooping lashes under,
    A pirate lurks, the heart's sweet freight to plunder,
And then to cast adrift the ravished prize.

Still, like a cloud, sun-kissed to dazzling dyes,
And by the glory blotted from the skies,
    I revel in her rays;—yet who can wonder!
        She smiles on me.

I know the swift and deadly lightning lies
Behind the snowy curtains' deep disguise;
    I know the shackled and imprisoned thunder,
    Will rend its mute environments asunder,
But love above all overthrow shall rise—
        She smiles on me.

13

'TIS ALL FOR THEE.

'TIS all for thee—the wild unrest,
   The dream-bird's song in slumber's nest,
   The rapture glowing through disguise
   When in my clasp thy soft palm lies,
And love stands silently confessed.

My heart has but one welcome guest,
With one fond feeling is oppressed,
   For when it sings and when it sighs,
            'Tis all for thee.

When like a low wind from the west
That breathes the prayer it knoweth best,
   Impassioned melodies arise
   From love's sweet lute—when longing eyes
Droop with a melting, mute request,
            'Tis all for thee.

I DO NOT CARE.

I DO not care—thy chosen path pursue,
These are some foolish whisperings to rue,
Some idle hopes and tokens to recall,
But that is all—
And thorns may thicken where the lilies grew.

And yet what shafts of passion melted through
Thine eyes' wild witchery and wondrous blue!
Still, if cold gloom must on their glory fall,
I do not care.

Nay, sweet one, whisper softly thou art true,
And with these dimpled hands in mine, renew
Love's tender thrall;
Pluck not the roses from life's barren wall,
Nor thus with ashes strew—ah well! adieu;
I do not care.

'TIS BUT A TEAR.

'TIS but a tear, still in its mute embrace
    A weeping sorrow veils her weary face:
    It is a hope, a prayer, a wild regret,
    A cenotaph for starry dreamings set,
A wandering drop from passion's broken vase.

It is a mantle shielding frail disgrace,
An alkahest for noble and for base   .
    When grief or disappointment comes—and yet
    'Tis but a tear.

It is a gem which lights the dimpled face
When rapture rides the heart his frantic race;
    A scimeter in azure eyes, or jet,
    Whose argument no man hath ever met;
A sword whose bright edge leaves nor scar nor trace—
    'Tis but a tear.

AH ME!

AH me! ah me!—whence comes the low refrain?
  I heard it erstwhile—hark! Ah me!—again.
  I feel the tingling blood in pity sweep
  Along my veins; and still the tidings creep
Upon the darkness like a funeral strain.

There is the muffled death-roll of the rain
Upon the icy rampart of the pane,
  But through it drifts a diapason deep—
    Ah me! Ah me!

Is love unfaithful that the hours complain?
Doth some gray phantom haunt the night amain?
  It is the voice of griefs that may not sleep,
  The dirge of days who for their errors weep,
For love is vanity, devotion vain—
    Ah me! Ah me!

LOOK UP.

LOOK up, my pet—look to the open sky,
    Turn like a violet thy slumbrous eye
    Unto the clustered stars, and thou shalt see
    The measure of the love I bear for thee—
           Nay, do not sigh;

If men have faithless been in days gone by,
Still to my pleadings grant a sweet reply;
    Shed all the gracious light of love on me—
           Look up, my pet.

There is no fate my soul would not defy
That on this breast thy gentle head might lie,
    For in my life thy presence still must be
             Its mystery
Eternally—and wilt thou still deny?
           Look up, my pet.

FOREVER TRUE.

FOREVER true, my heart must cleave and cling
    Unto its cross of love and suffering:
It still must bloom, its weary life renew
        With tears for dew,
And sighs for breezes blown from sorrow's wing.

What solace may the fragrant breath of spring
Unto a dead or painted lily bring!
    Or to a heart that dreams its lone life through,
        Forever true!

What care I that the birds of summer sing,
And blossom-bells their chimes of perfume ring!
    I only know that eyes so fond to woo,
        So deeply blue,
Are shrouded, and my heart is—broken thing—
        Forever true.

WHEN I WAS YOUNG.

WHEN I was young, and sweet hopes hung
Like blooms the dewy hours among,
   A wandering minstrel softly stole
   Into a corner of my soul,
And nestling there, divinely sung.

Weird strains of music from his tongue
Were sweetly breathed or wildly flung,
      And love was life's enchanted goal
            When I was young.

But now the harp to which I clung
Is mute, dismantled, and unstrung ;
      The minstrel's songs no longer roll
      From out my bosom's frozen pole,
And all the hopes are dead that sprung
            When I was young.

20

JUST SWEET SIXTEEN.

JUST sweet sixteen, with hair of sunshine rolled
   In many a flossy flake and flame of gold,
     And cheeks through which enchanted roses press
     A dim suspicion of the tenderness
               Their bloom enfold.

She loved, alas! a youth as poor and bold
As any youth who loved in days of old;
     Ah! she was fondly foolish, I confess,
              Just sweet sixteen.

Then came a suitor with a wealth untold,
Who craved her tender charms to have and hold,
     And he was sixty—rather more than less—
     Still, with a sigh, the maiden murmured "yes."
Knowest thou the maiden soul and body sold—
              Just sweet sixteen?

IT WAS A DREAM.

IT was a dream, but from the golden day
  It turns full many a sunny shaft away,
    And solemnly its spectral presence swings
    On dusky, dim, and omnipresent wings,
Above my life, like some grim bird of prey.

What boots it that I petulantly say,
When gloried over with the noon's red ray,
    And human fellowship its valor brings,
                  " It was a dream !"

I saw the tawny moon-tide sweep and sway
Athwart a maiden's charming cheek of May,
    And when I sighed unutterable things
    And wooed her in the glad stars' glitterings,
The odor of her lips' sweet rose was Nay!—
                  It was a dream.

22

SCATTER THE SHADOWS.

THOUGH time with drastic silent surge
  Sweeps graveward all the human race ;
The darkest wave it may up-urge
  Is lighted by some smiling face.

  Philosophy or faith will chase
The shadows from life's outer verge,
Though time with drastic silent surge
  Sweeps graveward all the human race.

Then let us from dim doubt emerge
  Into the light of love's sweet grace,
And let the dolor of the dirge
  Unto a joyous song give place,
Though time with drastic silent surge
  Sweeps graveward all the human race.

MIGNONETTE.

HAZEL-EYED maiden, Mignonette,
　　Harken the tale I would o'er-tell,
　The lesson my heart hath learned so well
From love's alluring alphabet.

Never can I the smile forget
　　Which over my life in splendor fell—
Hazel-eyed maiden, Mignonette,
　　Harken the tale I would o'er-tell.

Songs of the sea must ever fret
　　The pearly throat of the haunted shell,
　　But love's are the only sweets that swell
From the lips of my perfumed "dainty pet,"
Hazel-eyed maiden, Mignonette.

WHICH SHALL IT BE?

"WHICH shall it be," the maiden sighed,
    "The heart of love, or the hand of gold?
The gaunt wolf roams in the wintry wold,
And the sea of years moans wild and wide!"

Ah! poverty plays on the harp of pride,
    And the world is dark and the world is cold—
"Which shall it be," the maiden sighed,
    "The heart of love, or the hand of gold?"

The wave of want is a bitter tide,
    Whose saddest wrecks are still untold,
    For grief wraps silence, fold on fold,
O'er the story death shall wholly hide—
"Which shall it be," the maiden sighed,
    "The heart of love, or the hand of gold?"

NOTHING.

"WHAT are your thoughts, my pretty maid?"
   "O nothing," she replied,
The while her cheeks in red arrayed
   The soft response denied;

For there are tricks in every trade,
   But love hath naught to hide;
"What are your thoughts, my pretty maid?"
   "O nothing," she replied.

A footstep wandered down the glade,
   A footstep as of pride,
And all her soul with sweets was swayed
   When he stood at her side:
"What are your thoughts, my pretty maid?"
   "O nothing," she replied.

26

WHICH WERE THE BETTER?

THE heart may break, the heart may bend,
    Bend or break with a tear or sigh—
Which were the better in the end?

Droop with a love in silence penned,
    Sink with the sorrow of good-by:
The heart may break, the heart may bend.

Wearily over the world to wend,
    Or under a marble slab to lie—
Which were the better in the end?

Cold the clasp of a treasured friend,
    And wintry shadows haunt her eye;
The heart may break, the heart may bend.

Doubts and fears my bosom rend;
　　To sue sweet favor or to fly—
Which were the better in the end?

I plead unto the stars, who send
　　But mocking echo in reply:
"The heart may break, the heart may bend—
Which were the better in the end?"

SWEET, SAD LOVE.

"THE sweet sad love that mortals know"—
    So sighs the pine, so sobs the fir—
"Is but a jewel set in woe;

"It is the soul of winds that blow
    Around the crumbling sepulcher,
The sweet, sad love that mortals know;

"And e'en the fond heart's overflow,
    And tearful wish for days that were,
Is but a jewel set in woe.

"A maiden sings our boughs below
    And wooes, her dreamy eyes aver,
The sad, sweet love that mortals know;

"She cannot deem in hope's rich glow
    That passion, newly born to her,
Is but a jewel set in woe.

" And thus, forever, sad and slow
    Our muffled strings to sorrow stir :
The sad, sweet love that mortals know
Is but a jewel set in woe."

THE LAMENT OF THE REJECTED.

IF she must be another's blushing bride,
                    Perhaps 'tis best :
The world which once was gracious still is wide.

Yet gloomily a grief will ever hide
                    Within my breast,
If she must be another's blushing bride :

While hope, foregoing all for which she sighed,
                    Shall banish rest ;
The world which once was gracious still is wide.

And but a wreck my soul will rock, and ride
                    On sorrow's crest,
If she must be another's blushing bride.

31

FIXED SHADOWS.

Ah me ! that love should find at eventide
> No waiting nest !
The world which once was gracious still is wide.

Then let regret put on the plume of pride
> And make new quest,
If she must be another's blushing bride !
The world which once was gracious still is wide.

WOOING IS BAD.

WHICH is the best to woo,
   Tell me, I pray,
Brown eyes, or black, or blue—
Which is the best to woo?
Which will dead love renew,
   Hazel or gray?
Which is the best to woo?
   Tell me, I pray.

Wooing is bad at best,
   Sweet though it be;
Nay, fairest, smooth thy crest,
Wooing *is* bad at best;
Love's is a brittle nest
   In a glass tree;
Wooing is bad at best,
   Sweet though it be.

ONLY A ROSEBUD.

ONLY a rosebud red,
      As a heart token,
Scentless now, sere and dead,
Only a rosebud red,
Like to the hope it sped,
      Blighted and broken;
Only a rosebud red,
      As a heart token.   .

SHADOWS.

THE sun sinks, and shadows mute and gray
                    Like ghosts upstart!
And mutinous memory holds despotic sway
When the sun sinks, and shadows mute and gray
Steal from the trailing drapery of day
                    Into my heart.
Ah! the sun sinks, and shadows mute and gray
                    Like ghosts upstart.

BLUE EYES.

BLUE eyes, whose curtains fall
        Over their glory !
What heart cannot recall
Blue eyes whose curtains fall
        On love's sweet story !
Shielding, yet showing all,
Blue eyes, whose curtains fall
        Over their glory.

IN THE MAY WEATHER.

UNDER dim twilight skies
　　　　In the May weather,
Soft pleas and sweet replies,
Under dim twilight skies,
Waken to lips and eyes
　　　　Wedded together,
Under dim twilight skies
　　　　In the May weather.

YOUTH'S DREAM.

"O HEAVENLY dream!" a fair youth sighed,
  As 'mongst the buds and blooms that twine
 Their beauties in love's red sunshine
A vision nestled, gracious-eyed,
Out-wafting witchcraft far and wide
  From look and parted lips divine—
"O dream, no future shall divide,"
  Said he, "thy loving heart and mine!"

But when the youth about his prize,
  Enraptured, eager arms had thrown,
The wild light faded from his eyes,
  The rapture from his heart was flown;
For reft of passion's sweet disguise,
  The burden that he bore was stone.

LEE.

OUT from the battle's wreck of pride and plume,
   And all the midnight of mad overthrow.
The chieftain strode, as heroes must who grow
The grander for an atmosphere of gloom :
Came with a soul unrifled of the bloom
   Which faith and courage marry to bestow :
   Came back to love which was a crown to woe
A garland for his sorrow and his tomb.

And when his rigid icy hands were crossed
   Above the big brave heart forever hushed,
      So warm a heart became so cold a stone
The people pondered but on what he lost
   When from his brow the drooping bay was brushed,
      And in his greater grief forgot their own.

BALLADE OF DECEITFUL WOMAN.

IT happened in the balmy spring,
    When perfumes fresh and rare
Dripped from the brooding twilight's wing
    Upon the drowsy air;
    And she, Kathleen, was young and fair
As dreams of fancy's weaving,
    And I thought not, in passion's glare,
That woman is deceiving.

My little one, I said, I bring
    Sweet hope to speed my prayer,
The while her cheeks were blossoming
    With love-buds waving there:
    O she was fond and debonair
Beyond cold art's achieving,
    And in my heart there was no care
That woman is deceiving.

Sweetest, I said, this golden ring
    On thy white finger wear;
See how my lightest kisses cling
    Like rose-leaves to thy hair!
    Come to my soul, I said, and share
Life's gladness and its grieving,
    Unthoughful in love's charming snare
That woman is deceiving.

Envoy.

Ah, prince! we are a happy pair,
    Too happy for believing;
And in my rapture I forswear
    That woman is deceiving.

BALLADE OF COUNTRY PLACES.

HEARKEN the sad recital of my woes
    That will not brook concealment in my breast,
For even now the dermis of my nose
    Is peeling off and powdering my vest ;
    Perhaps when my misfortunes are confessed
This wild disgust may lose its sharpest traces ;
    But heed my warning—be no summer guest
        At country places.

Said I, last August, How the hot sun glows !
    The very air is with the glare oppressed.
O for the fields, I said, where piping crows
    Build in the daffodils their stately nest.
    Wherefore I left the city, traveling west,
And plunged into the greenwood's airs and graces,
    My bosom full of dreams of grateful rest
        In country places.

FIXED SHADOWS.

Alas! alas! no milk nor honey flows,
    Nor fresh eggs tarry where I made my quest;
The bony farmer said, "Sich projuce goes
    For them rich city fellers to digest."
    Meanwhile, the sun made up his mind to test
The staying quality of human faces,
    And my poor nose put on a crimson crest,
        In country places.

ENVOY.

Ah, prince! a thousand insects, bad at best,
    Along my back ran mad and frantic races;
And things that move live only to molest
        In country places.

BALLADE OF THE COLD SEA.

THE breeze was balmy and the sea was blue,
    And morning into blossoms kissed the spray,
When gallantly a blithe and merry crew
    Into the frozen ocean sailed away.
    Ah! little recked they of the piercing day
When phantom icy fingers would bestow
    The last sad rite and wrap the rigid clay
In cerement and sepulcher of snow.

Familiar home-scenes faded out of view,
    And winter smote the faded cheeks of May,
But onward still the bark, to duty true,
    Into the frozen ocean sailed away.
    The wild wind shrieked, the sky hung leaden gray,
The clouds shook out their fatal dust below,
    And in the shrouds a hoarse fate seemed to say,
"In cerement and sepulcher of snow."

FIXED SHADOWS.

His black, bleak mantle cruel midnight threw
    Athwart the sinking sun's last rosy ray,
And clasped in chill embrace the brave men who
    Into the frozen ocean sailed away.
    No day-beam on the gloom made bold to stray,
And Hope herself forsook the haunt of woe :
    Ah me ! "God pity them," we can but pray,
"In cerement and sepulcher of snow."

ENVOY.

A gallant crew, with banners streaming gay,
Into the frozen ocean sailed away ;
But now they rest—ah well !—the angels know,
In cerement and sepulcher of snow.

BALLADE OF THE GOLDEN WEST.

"GOOD-BY, my darling," the young man cries;
    "Good-by till I build thee the dearest nest
In the land of soft Hesperian skies,
    In the golden solitudes of the west."
    The maid to her true-love's heart is pressed,
And into her eye the quick tear leaps;
    But when he is gone o'er the hill's dim crest
She foldeth her empty arms, and weeps.

Full many a blithesome token hies
    To gladden the maiden's eager breast,
And whisper of love's unbroken ties
    In the golden solitudes of the west.
    But when on her warm and rosy rest
The cold pale oaf of absence sweeps,
    And doubt is her heart's unbidden guest,
She foldeth her empty arms, and weeps.

FIXED SHADOWS.

The years drift by like lingering sighs,
    Like deep-drawn sighs from an age's chest,
For the maiden's heart, like a crushed rose, lies
    In the golden solitudes of the west;
    And hope flies forth on a fruitless quest,
For mystery over the dead hush sleeps,
    And the maiden forgets "God knoweth best,"
She foldeth her empty arms, and weeps.

Envoy.

The maiden may find no alkahest
In the golden solitudes of the west,
But over a mound, where ivy creeps,
She foldeth her empty arms, and weeps.

SHIFTING SHADOWS.

THAUMATURGUS.

I.

WHAT is the reason of the snow
    Fluttering flower-like down below,
Out of a mystic realm opaque
Where no star-beam brightens a break?
What is the reason of its fall
White and clean from an ashen pall?
Why not quiver, and whirl, and float,
Out of a cloud cup's crystal throat?
Why not fairily slide and slip
Over the winter's glittering lip,
Rather than meek, and soft, and dumb,
Out of the womb of gloom to come?

II.

Why should the vanquished ice-god fling
Magical wafts from his bitter wing,

Quickening earth to fragrant deeds
And wooing the wastes to bourgeoning
 Where the luminous line of snow recedes?
Why should he challenge the sun to bring
 A glory wherever his footstep leads?
Yet ever the daintiest buds emerge
From the folds of the fading winter's surge,
And birds their tenderest anthems sing
In the hush that follows the dead year's dirge,
 And heralds the dimpled spring.

III.

What is the impulse glad and wise,
Who is the angel in disguise,
 Scattering wreaths of sweetest flowers
 Over the ashes of the hours?
What is the force that underlies
All our wonderful love implies?
Love, that like a violet grows
Out of the couchings of the snows,
Love that bends like the lily, prayer,
Over the dim rim of despair;
Who is the spirit of the spell?
Harken, and let thine own heart tell.

IV.

Love is the secret, love the power,
Changing the snow-flake to the flower,
Purging the mad heart's bitter well
Into a heavenly hydromel;
Love on the earth, or love above,
Still wherever, 'tis only love.
Love it is that strews the snow
    Out of a leaden waste of sky,
Only to teach that brooding woe,
    Breaks into blossoms by and by,
Only that we may better know
    The rest which waiteth on a sigh.

UNFINISHED.

I.

FROM out the years obscure, remote,
Unfinished song on shadowy wings
Across my life forever float,
And brush from love's abandoned strings
Their saddest note.

II.

I catch the sweet familiar strain
Which first through life's fair temple swept,
But silence grasps it back again,
And nothing fills my soul, except
A weary pain.

III.

The night winds, as they murmur by,
    Bring e'er some isolated link,
Some fragment from the wrecks that lie
    Within the past, then sadly sink
          Into a sigh.

IV.

How oft my fond heart makes pursuit,
    When, through the dark boughs of the firs,
A faint voice like a spirit flute
    The starry hush of midnight stirs,
          Then all is mute.

V.

How often, when the moonbeams play
    With shadows in the wilderness,
I fancy in some graceful ray,
    The flutter of a phantom dress,
          Long passed away!

VI.

Thus through the dim rifts of the years,
 But broken chords of memory rise,
And fancy, deeming that she hears
  The olden songs, uplift her eyes
    Through heavy tears.

VII.

And life must, like a statue, stand
 Half wrought in fate's grim studio,
An outline of a poem planned
  By hope which perished 'neath a blow
    Of sorrow's hand.

WAITING.

I.

WHERE booms the blue Atlantic on its beaches
    In bright, revolving reaches,
  And, like a sighing nun,
The oak in mossy veiling, dusk and dun,
Her musical sweet creed forever teaches
    Beside the singing sea,
I sought for hope and love, and found despair and thee·

II.

The cedars hung their deep-hued banners o'er us,
    The billows broke before us,
    And tenderly at rest
Thy golden head lay pillowed on my breast,
Until so bitter fate asunder tore us,
    And bade the years sweep by
On wings that waft my soul a song that is a sigh.

III.

I gave thee back no sweet and tender token,
    Love's links are all unbroken,
    Its plighted troth is true;
And, though disparted, fondly I renew
The sacred compact in the star-shine spoken,
    And bide the golden hour
When in my life shall bloom love's first and fairest flower.

TO IDA.

I.

GENTLE maiden, maiden pure,
    Maiden dove-eyed and demure,
From the soul's most golden censer
    Graven to thy portraiture,
Waft I tenderness intenser
    Than I mutely may endure.

II.

When the night's soft hands unbar
    Dreamy hours, crepuscular;
When the wing of twilight hovers
    In the silence faint and far,
Love but only thee discovers,
    Smiling on me as a star.

III.

When the warm winds in the pine
 Sing a lullaby divine,
Or in low sonatas tremble
 Where the wreathing roses twine,
Still their sweetest tones resemble
 But the melody of thine.

IV.

In the lily, in the dew,
 In the violet's dear hue,
I can read but love's fond tidings
 Breathing all their beauty through,
And the midnight's hushed confidings
 E'er thy wooing voice renew.

V.

In thy bright and gracious eyes
 Elfin love in ambush lies,
And his arrow, swift and certain,
 With a sudden rapture flies
Through the fringes of the curtain
 Drooping o'er the fond disguise;

VI.

And the ruthless, roving lance
From the quiver of thy glance,
With a pang a sigh discloses,
Wounds the bosom it enchants,
And my heart, in chains of roses
At thy feet, a captive, pants.

THE COTTONWOOD SCOURGE.

I.

BY the banks of the turgid Klamath,
   In the shadow of snowy peaks,
A pestilence swings on implacable wings,
And horribly seeks, through the wearisome weeks,
   Fresh food for its hungerings.

II.

In the pine, in the fir, in the cedar,
   In the multiple tongues of the night,
There is ever a moan near akin to a groan,
And silence itself has a sorrow its own
   For the souls that have sailed out of sight.

III.

The plash of the rain on the window,
   The feathery flight of the snow,
The moonbeams that drift through the luminous rift
Of the cloud-rack—all tenderly, tearfully lift
   Their voices in threnodes of woe.

IV.

I stand in the city of silence,
   In the acre of broken hearts,
And deem that I hear in the fall of a tear
The music that thrills on an angel's ear
   When the golden life cord parts.

V.

And the dusky plumes of the pine-trees
   With a sad, soft anthem sigh—
A melody sung by no human tongue,
From the harp of death by a cold hand flung
   To those who yet must die.

VI.

And the past and present and future
    Are blent in a single tone—
An isolate note from a ghostly throat,
That over a new mound seems to float,
    And whiten into a stone.

VII.

By the banks of the turgid Klamath,
    Where the snow-browed peaks upshoot,
A sad-eyed care upon the air,
Like the soul of a deep, unspoken prayer,
    Broods eloquent and mute.

AN EMPTY NECROPOLIS.

I.

GRIEF etches on the marble-lidded tombs,
　　With tears for tools, an epitaph of woe;
He works in silence where the willow-plumes
　Rain sighs and shadows on the hush below,
While through the trailing surge of cypress glooms
　The stars, like great death-diamonds, sadly glow,
And hope and patient love—poor human things—
Above the icy ashes fold their wings.

II.

Like muffled chords from some grand organ flying
　A fugue of souls through time's cathedral sweeps.
Among the arches of the dim years dying—
　The arches where immortal echo weeps—

And constantly the mute are multiplying
  Where silence o'er her treasure vigil keeps,
And day by day the solemn mourners tread
The grassless path down-beaten for the dead.

III.

But in the heart there is a vacant acre
  Which gentle charity hath set aside,
Wherein she broods, an idle undertaker,
  And prays the death of doubt, and hate, and pride;—
Still on the beach the blue rush of the breaker
  Strews only lovely ruin, wild and wide,
While malice, envy, error, cunning, crime,
Sport with the storms, and scoff the toils of time.

IV.

Within her park the lovely sexton pineth
  Beneath the scowl of Eidolon despair,
For o'er her paths the rank weed proudly twineth
  And strews fierce blossoms on her whitened hair;
She looks above, but scarce a wan star shineth
  Between the sullen cloud-racks gathered there,
And by her gates the sable death-carts wind
With fair dead children of the human mind.

V.

What speeds detraction on its mad excursion?
　　What weights the wing of commendation down?
Why falls like lead the feather of aspersion?
　　Why floats like foam approval's golden crown?
What beam more fleet than whispers of aversion!
　　What snail so dilatory as renown!
For living hearts still bear the steel's cold thrust,
While garlands deck the dumb, unconscious dust.

VI.

What boot life's homilies and pure epistles
　　That plead unto the clod-encrusted soul!
The henbane of the heart, its thorns and thistles,
　　Still gather dew from passion's brimming bowl,
And hold high carnival though winter whistles
　　From out adversity's inclement pole,
But charity sobs at the ingleside
Above her graves, o'ergrown, unoccupied.

TO MRS. HATTIE STEWART.

I.

I WOULD that as an eagle throws
His image from the sky,
Or as the petal of a rose
Is wafted from its sweet repose
By some Eolian sigh,
The wraith of destiny may fling
But truant shadows from his wing
To pass, unpausing, by.

II.

I would that Love may richly dew
Thy life with pleasure's wine,
And spare thy cup the bitter rue
With which he maddened mine;
May time be golden, hearts be true;
May starry footsteps twinkle through

68

The garden of thy years,
And scatter blooms, and fond perfumes,
And music as of Pity's plumes,
Beguiling Sorrow's tears.

III.

I would that as the seasons sink
Into the mute unknown,
Some gentle memory may link
My name to Friendship's throne;
I would that I might dream, or think,
When brooding and alone,
That one bright bubble on the brink
Of thought were all my own.

IV.

I wish the spirits of the air.
And earth, and fire, and sea,
To crown thy soul's most silent prayer,
And from thy footsteps sweep despair,
Where'er thy path may be.
I would that peace, and love, and rest.
May make thy heart their common nest,
And all things beautiful and best,
I wish for thine and thee.

THE ICONOCLAST.

I.

A SWEEP of midnight hair—an eye whose glory
Is flashed from out the furnace of the soul—
A tongue attuned to love's sweet oratory—
Red lips writ o'er with kisses as a scroll;
And so you have the hero of my story:
No sallow saint; no priest in cowl and stole;
A common mortal twenty-six and past,
Unmarried, wealthy, an iconoclast.

II.

As breathes a sighing night-wind through the willow,
As to the pine a plaintive murmur clings,
As on the beach the blue, incessant billow
Its minor minstrelsy forever flings,
A tender longing o'er the young man's pillow
Outspread the sleepless shadow of its wings,

70

And launched him forth on Passion's painted ships
To gather fruit that withered on his lips.

III.

A tourist first, unto the thousand-citied
    And rosy Orient his fancy led :
Ascended mountains where the frost-loom knitted
    A shroud about their summits cold and dead ;
Then to the haunt of fig and palm tree flitted,
    Where history and legend weirdly wed,
And wooed Cleopatra where star-beams smile
Along the myth-wreathed waters of the Nile.

IV.

To Missolonghi, where were snapped asunder
    The golden strings of Byron's fierce, sweet lyre ;
To Africa, whose mute wastes quiver under
    The tawny lash of Fate's remorseless fire ;
And much saw he whereat to gaze and wonder,
    But in his soul there lurked a wild desire,
A nameless longing, deepest when he sighed,
That travel eased not, nothing satisfied.

V.

Along the dimpled disk of seas he drifted
    Before the waft of wanton kissing gales,
While flossy shreds and flakes of sunlight sifted
    From out the milky mystery of sails,
And phantom knights their spectral lances lifted
    In pale defiance over ghostly grails.
But still the youth, upon the wave's blue page,
No secret found his longing to assuage.

VI.

Then northward, where the fair Aurora's tresses,
    O'er-flecked with stars, bestrew the throbbing sky;
Where Hecla looms o'er icy wildernesses
    And proudly flaunts his crimson plume on high;
Where winter's thrall the fettered sea oppresses,
    And human bones the cold stars underlie:
O'er blinking floes that cling about the pole
He chased the fleeting fancies of the soul.

VII.

Then sought he peace in toil, it little mattered
    The nature or the name of the pursuit;

His first fair dream was as a fragrance scattered—
    The tree of travel bore but ashen fruit;
And so he desperately smote and shattered
    The idle image, smote it branch and root,
And sought in commerce and in cent per cent
The magical elixir of content.

VIII.

Swift argosies upon his pleasure waited
    With white wings bent above the purple tide,
Before whose flight the fierce typhoon abated,
    And Zephyr but a perfumed pinion plied.
Yet he was weary, disappointed, sated,
    And o'er the pyramids of gold he sighed,
For in the honey of his proud success
Still lurked the haunting, hollow bitterness.

IX.

And so he struck the idol into ashes,
    And sought nepenthe at another shrine :
Plunged headlong in the opal flood that flashes
    A languid lethe from its depths divine,

And kissed the siren from whose dreamy lashes
　　Streams out the glory and the gloom of wine:
Then to the phantom clung he close and fast,
Conceiving he had found the balm at last.

X.

But as the months the fevered weeks succeeded,
　　And nights of singing ushered days of sighs;
When time went limping by, or sped unheeded,
　　And sleep was torture in a mad disguise;
When life's fair bloom, with white lips, mutely pleaded
　　For one unsullied dew-drop from the skies—
The wretched youth, with giant heave and thrust,
O'erthrew the carnal idol in the dust.

XI.

About the shattered cup he lingered sadly,
　　As o'er a dream too fair so soon to fade,
And in a fond regret forgot how madly
　　His sweetest hope was flattered and betrayed:
Then reason swept the glowing fragments, gladly,
　　Into a grave which Iron Will had made;
While o'er the wreck she wrapped, and tucked, and tied
The pall-like mantles of remorse and pride.

XII.

We leave our sins with footstep undecided,
　　With backward stolen glance and frequent sigh;
But when from virtue we are once divided,
　　To folly's arms we run, we rush, we fly!
For man's strange destiny was ever guided
　　By hidden forces, wrenching it awry,
And all of us some sweet misdeeds pursue,
Forsaking old ones but to chase the new.

XIII.

From wine he wandered to the gaming-table,
　　Where men with pallid cheeks and eyes of glass
Sat statue-like amidst the heated Babel,
　　To lose or win, to scatter or amass,
And whether fortunate or not, unable
　　The tempting tonic of the cup to pass;
For men who hazard ever fondly think
To ride like bubbles on the beaker's brink.

XIV.

His horses all competitors outspeeded,
　　His yacht was foremost of a gallant fleet:
Success success in golden waves succeeded,
　　And fortune's favors fluttered to his feet:

But in these triumphs there was something needed
    To qualify the universal sweet—
A lacking flavor which his heart well knew
Its loneliness and longing would subdue.

XV.

And then the painted image, wrought so newly,
    Was petulantly from its altar spurned;
For o'er some dim and undiscovered thule,
    His restless spirit passionately yearned—
Some tryst to which, still tenderly and truly,
    His heart in hungry expectation turned;
Some mystic spot within whose peaceful gloom,
The rose of rest distills her rare perfume.

XVI.

Thus many fragile idols were erected,
    Insanely worshiped, fiercely overthrown;
But, hoping still, the dauntless youth selected
    Another image wrought of sober stone,
Yet in whose searching eye his soul detected
    A kindred light to that within his own—
A falcon glance, with never-folded wings,
Which soared o'er great and swooped to little things.

XVII.

For Science now engaged his rapt attention,
    And on its wondrous pinion Thought took flight,
And hung with studious and hushed suspension
    Among the dimmest distances of night,
Or swept with swift and subtile apprehension
    The veil of tangled theories from sight,
Nor knew he pause, nor daliance, nor rest,
Until he lay on nature's vanquished breast.

XVIII.

With all the gracious sisterhood of flowers—
    The bleeding-heart, the pink, the eglantine—
He held sweet converse, couching in the bowers,
    And dreaming dreams as fleeting as divine—
Strange dreams that woke him in the starry hours,
    And thrilled along his veins like purple wine;
Prophetic dreams that from the future stole
The shadows of the wish within his soul.

XIX.

To him the tulip hung atilt with meaning,
    The jasmine breathed sweet creeds upon the air:
The milk-skinned lily on the swart rose leaning,
    Was to his heart a promise and a prayer;

While fancy 'mongst the blossoms went a-gleaning,
    And garnered sheaves of heavenly beauty there:
Yet in it all there hid a mystic lore
Whose depths he struggled vainly to explore.

XX.

And then he drew with tender indecision
    A veil about the image, but forbore
To smite it with the turbulent derision
    Upheaped on idols loved and left before,
For in the flow'rets dwelt a dreamy vision
    Whose blooming face a wreath of promise wore,
And to his heart its blue eyes seemed to say
That he should clasp his crown some happy day.

XXI.

And next he woke the mystery that slumbers
    In musing Poesy's o'er-blossomed strings;
Brimmed up the summer night with wooing numbers,
    And rained rich melody from fancy's wings,
While every icy fetter that encumbers
    The heart notes, in their wilder flutterings,
He swept aside, and soaring far and free,
Shook out the carols of his ecstasy.

XXII.

And then one night a maiden stood before him,
    With love's rich bloom upon her peerless lips,
Who flashed a thrill of sudden rapture o'er him
    From eyes unused to sorrow's sad eclipse—
Unclouded seas of azure that upbore him
    Upon their blue, as ocean bears her ships,
And, in their dazzling depths, reposed the gem
Which crowned his life's unfinished diadem.

XXIII.

As on a drifting cloud a star impinges,
    Translating all its blackness into bloom;
As morning with a kiss of crimson tinges
    The marble of an isolated tomb,
The maiden's eyes behind their silken fringes
    Shone out upon the poet's life of gloom,
And lighting up the shadows, grim and gray,
Swept with a smile the long unrest away.

XXIV.

And when the autumn came with golden flushes,
    And rich-hued tracery of leaf and sky,
In murmured vows and palpitating hushes,
    The twinkling twilights stole in rapture by;

While, on the maiden's cheek, the conscious blushes
    Were to the lover's plea a fond reply,
Then on the pillow of his constant breast,
The Idol of his life and love lay pressed.

*   *   *   *   *

XXV.

And here we leave him to his own resources,
    In proud possession of his charming bride,
A candidate for quarrels and divorces,
    And all the wretched rest of it beside;
For true love runs in but contracted courses
    Since marriage knots so carelessly are tied
That Hymen, with his air most cool and polished,
Suggests that nuptial nonsense be abolished.

XXVI.

We leave the lady, too, with white arms twining
    About her husband, handsome, brave, and true;
And yet we part reluctantly, divining
    What racy single combats will ensue—
What snaps and snarls! what petulant repining!
    And broomstick battles! Yes, we sadly rue
The parting, but 'twill always be the same;
She'll change the trouble with a change of name.

XXVII.

And so the story, carried to conclusion,
    Would blossom to a wild, fantastic play,
Its moral, chaos, and its plot, confusion,
    Its heroes, husbands deftly put away,
Its heroines, a beautiful illusion,
    Its epilogue the trump of judgment-day:
We therefore o'er the scene a curtain draw,
And leave the happy pair to love—and law.

LAQUELLE?

MERRY eyes, now gray, now blue,
　　Yearning, laughing, tender, true;
　Lips as red as rarest roses
Orient garden ever grew,
　　Velvet cheeks whose bloom discloses
Eden's fairest charms anew;
Luscious maid I love so well,
Young and beautiful—laquelle?

In the wind's song, wild and free,
Sings no voice so sweet to me
　　As the sigh her thoughts compel,
　　Broken sighs and soft that tell
Every tender ecstasy—
　　Loved and lovely maid—laquelle?

THE PHANTOM BARQUE.

I.

UPON an island in the sea of time
    I watched, and waited :
And presently, from out some starry clime,
    From out the years, with love and passion freighted,
Across the rolling reach of tides sublime
    A sail appeared. Oh! how the moments grated
O'er harsh impediments, with dull delay,
Until the barque was anchored in the bay.

II.

Then stole a wondrous maid my senses o'er,
    As in my dreaming
Full often had she sweetly swept before,
    Her tropic tresses prodigally streaming,
Like sunshine washing some celestial shore ;
    And I fell down and worshiped, fondly deeming

That in the hazel rapture of her eye
No love could languish, no devotion die.

III.

The days rushed by like rubies, brief and bright,
    Like pearls outscattered
By gentle angels in ecstatic flight:
    And then, alas! Disaster shook her tattered
And gloomy banner to the weeping night,
    While winds of desolation smote and shattered
The brittle fabric of my love and trust,
And whirled its starry fragments in the dust.

*   *   *   *   *

IV.

Upon the isle, the lone and silent isle,
    I still am biding;
And gazing o'er the watery wastes I smile
    To find my heart with hope its dreams dividing—
The dreary hope, which time may not beguile,
    That if the radiant barque the waves be riding
In earth's remotest and most stormy sea,
It may come back, though but a wreck, to me.

TOLL THE BELL.

TOLL the bell, the iron-throated
    Bell despairful !
Let its tidings be outfloated,
    Sad and prayerful,
From each spire and dome and steeple,
As a warning to the people,
    As a voice from heaven sped :
As a note of tender pity
From the silence of the city
    Of the dead !

Toll ! And may its melancholy,
    Deep and solemn,
Crush the heart's incessant folly
    As a column !
May its clamor, far outreaching,
More than dreary wastes of preaching,

Peal at Pleasure's shrine,
Ever calling, and enthralling,
With an eloquence appalling,
Terrible, divine !

Yesterday the clay was glowing,
Now 'tis ashes !
And the cup of Fate, o'erflowing,
Grimly dashes
On the vital spark its wave—
Gloomy wave which ever lashes,
And in sullen silence plashes
On its shore, the grave !

Ah ! to live is oft to languish
And repine,
Since around our dreamings anguish
Must entwine ;
And the pale thing, named Hereafter,
From the dimpled lip of Laughter
Sweeps the summer bloom ;
While before his cold eye, Pleasure,
Casting down love's beaded measure,
Totters to the tomb.

Toll, O sexton ! Let thy muffled
    Dirge begin,
For another soul hath shuffled
    Off its sin.
Toll, O sexton, warped and bended,
From the dead old years descended,
    Toll thy monody !
For the next wild note that clashes
Over mute, dismantled ashes
    May be rung for thee !

FATE.

I.

SHE stands before me, but I cannot know
    The strange, swift lights that glow
    Within her great sad eyes,
That like the shifting and inconstant skies
Are masking ever in some weird disguise,
    Now beautifully blue,
And now like midnight, with fierce lightnings fusing
    through.

II.

Between the crimson cleavage of her lips
    A sigh full often slips,
    And shadows, gaunt and gray,
Across their bloom in wan procession stray,
Like death-bells tolling on a bridal-day—
    Like ghostly footed snows,
Whose crystal kisses blanch the blushes of the rose.

III.

I wander o'er the mountains and the tides
    Where'er her footstep guides;
    Through tangled, tender hours
That twine their blossoms in life's secret bowers,
And then into the wailing storm which lowers
    Along the patient years,
And on my soul outpours the tempest of its tears.

IV.

Through cloistered sorrow's sacristy she lingers
    Where cruel beaks and fingers
    My bleeding heart assail;
Then out into the fragrance-freighted gale—
Still on forever to the portal pale,
    Death's wan and waiting gate—
Whereto my guide conducts me, for her name is Fate.

REVERIES.

THE night is dark without; the sobbing rain
    Beats baffled at the spattered window pane,
Imploring, like some spirit of the night
A moment pausing in its starless flight
To pray admittance. So I sit, and think,
While in the blackened grate the bright coals wink
Suggestive, and I watch the golden stars
That from their dungeon, and its iron bars,
In shining troops depart.

   *   *   *   *   *

                Out from the aisles
Of some dim sanctuary gayly files
A bridal train, while roses underlie
Their footsteps fragrantly, and seem to sigh
A sacrificial blessing. Light of heart
They pass the sacred portal; tears may start,
And fall upon the rose-leaves, but they rise

Belit with smiles into the joyous eyes
That beam as bright as Venus in the skies.

*   *   *   *   *

I look out from the casement, and the rain
Beats baffled at the spattered window pane ;
I watch the sodden sky, the dripping night,
To see if still the sparks pursue their flight :
But all is dark ! The clouds bowl blackly by ;
The wind sweeps through the cedar with a sigh,
And in the dim expanse of heaven I see
No point of brightness which a spark might be.
Then to my sofa, and I sit and think,
While in the blackened grate the red coals wink
Prophetic, and each waving spire of flame
Becomes a monument, whereon no name
Is written.

*   *   *   *   *

        Down the hushed and solemn aisles
Of that dim sanctuary slowly files
A burial train. The roses still are there,
But bruised and broken ; and the thorns are bare
And brittle. Happy feet no fragrance press
From their dead leaves—and all is bitterness.

MY BOY.

I.

THEY say that he is dead—my baby boy,
 My little gentleman with flaxen tresses;
 Departed from these treasured-up caresses
Which I had thought so fondly to employ:
 Forever gone! while sad and empty dresses,
And here and there a consecrated toy
Are eloquent with such a mighty pain,
That he is wrested back from heaven again.

II.

A stranger closed his eyes, his deep blue eyes,
 So like to violets, and starry seas—
 A stranger drew the curtain over these,
While Death stood gloating o'er his ravished prize,
 Which, with his skeleton and brazen keys,
He had unlocked, and to the waiting skies

Let out the 'prisoned spirit, pure and white,
Which heavenward took its seraph-guided flight.

III.

It booteth not my lost one to repine,
    My loved, my little one no more forever!
    'Twere better I had known the darling never
Than thus the reaching heart-strings should entwine
    About a sword-like grief, which can but sever
The coiling tendrils from the bleeding vine :
And yet these arms of love, though cloven down,
Shoot out anew to clasp their sorrow's crown.

IV.

His footsteps patter through the solitude
    And dreary isolation of existence,
    With such a musical and soft insistence,
That from its loss my love is warped, and wooed,
    And wafted to that dim, delightful distance
Beyond the azure where the stars are strewed :
And like a bark on some celestial sea,
Affection anchors in eternity.

MISERERE.

WE stood in the glorious, golden dawn
    Of a new delightful day,
And the sunlight fell like a spirit spell
On the bonnie brown locks I love so well,
And I looked the devotion no tongue can tell,
    And a passion no pen portray.

O sweet was the dawn of that fair day,
    With its pendulous hopes a-bloom ;
But a tempest, apace, smote the heaven's fair face,
And brushed from the future all token and trace
Of wooing perfume, with its finger of gloom,
And wrought, with a terrible skill, in its place
    A tomb.

And now, in the desolate waste of years,
    In the desert of grief, I grope ;

For death unto distance yields cruel assistance.
And life is not life, it is merely existence,
While memory dashes swift tears o'er the ashes
    That bury the beacon of hope.

We stand in the gloom of some cold curse,
    In the palm of a pressing pain,
And I sigh for the birth of a happier morn,
When sunlight the bonnie brown locks may adorn;
Or else, that the sharpest and bitterest thorn
That grows o'er the head of the dear and the dead
    May rivet our hearts again.

THE HEART.

"O HEART!" the maiden cries, the sighing
      maiden ;
  "O chalice, sparkling over with delight !
Thou happy bird with ecstasy down-laden
    That makest music through the starry night !
    Thou buoyant bark, whose palpitating flight
Is guided on to love's delicious Aidenn !
O trusting heart ! O heart with joy oppressed,
Thou makest heavenly anguish in my breast."

"O loving heart ! Thou heart upheaped with roses !"
    A radiant mother softly murmurs this :
" O yearning heart, whose fond arm sweetly closes
    About its new-born rapture ! Heart of bliss,
    Thou couch, more downy than an angel's kiss,
Whereon my bright-eyed darling hushed reposes—

Rock gently, heart, within my joyous breast,
'The birdling slumbers in its swaying nest."

" O weary heart, in ashes unavailing !"
 A bended figure breathes : "O muffled tomb,
Above whose clay the kites of death are sailing
  To mark the ashen prey they shall consume !
  O sepulcher of life's most sweet perfume,
And grave of love ! Alas ! the day is failing,
And thou, O cruel heart, shalt yield me rest,
A broken thorn within an icy breast."

TO ATLANTA.

BUT yesterday the wild bird built her nest,
     And reared her brood of little ones, where now
Thy proudest monuments confine the hum
And hurry of a multitude.   Along
Thy busy marts, one thinks he almost hears
The music of the brook, which erstwhile ran
Discoursive through the flags and flowerets: and
At night, when muffled falls the footstep far
Of guardsman on his rounds, attentive ears
Can catch the echo of the robin's call,
And seem to hear the mottled partridge cry
Within his rosy fastnesses.   Anon
A spirit finger from the pine-harp's strings
An anthem sweepeth, and the forest sings
An undertone of melody.

The ax
Seems still to ring along thy thoroughfares,
Responsive to the brawny arm of toil;
And at the eventide thy flagstones bloom,
Or seem to bloom, with violets. The wheels
Of thy fast multiplying industries
Are garlanded with blossoms till they trail
Upon the highway, and the eager feet
Of energy press fragrance from their leaves,
Until thou might'st have been by magic built
Mysteriously in a single night
Upon a couch of flowers.

In the gloom
Thy temples cast, where browsed the deer,
And burrowed close the fleecy rabbit, now
The stately cedars nod their solemn plumes,
And guard like tireless sentinels the still
And sacred acre; while from slated spire
And heavenward-lifted dome, and chapel loft,
The mellow bells with silver voices call
To Christian worship.

With the whistle shrill
Of engines straining through thy throbbing heart

The winding horns of hunters seem to blend,
And as from startled hills the echoes come,
Imagination sees the stay in flight
Across the honeysuckled distance: there,
Excitedly in hot pursuit, the lank
And panting hounds; beyond, the riders—fast
They follow, and the forest wraps them in.
The drays upon the cobble-stones are but
The rattle of the horses on the plain,
And from the mountain falls a low refrain
Of winding horns, and all is hushed again.
Fair city of the south, God speed thee! may
Thy future be through blossoms hanging fair
And sweet athwart thy path. Child of the woods,
Thy proud escutcheon be the kingly oak
Whose throne within the virgin solitudes
Thy queenly arm o'erthrew, and in the wealth
Of thine unbraided tresses I would weave
This humble chaplet, for as blushed
The dove-eyed Venus from the lisping sea,
So from the chalice of the wild rose grew
Thy wondrous charms, Atlanta.

THE DOVE AND THE MAIDEN.

THE sad dove sits in her dim retreat
In the wildwood, hushed and lone,
And never a note is heard in her throat
Save now and anon a moan.
A light wing comes on the balmy air
And gladdens the waiting dove,
Then off to the hills and the glistening rills
She hies with her cooing love.

A maiden stands in the slanting glow
Of the amber-dripping west,
But not in her dreams are its yellow beams,
Nor the star with the crimson crest.
A footstep sounds on the gravel walk,
A footstep glad and free;
And the maiden can bide no thought beside,
"My darling comes back to me!"

THE FEVER.

I.

HE stood in the twilight as the stars
    Grew golden in the sky,
And never a word his pale lips stirred
    Save "Kiss me," and "Good by;"
Then she to her lonely grief, and he
    In the path where duty led—
To the city of graves and sobbing waves,
    The city of the dead.

II.

Rosy of cheek and strong of limb,
    And sturdy of heart was he;
But the yellow fiend's call was in hovel and hall,
And the city was wrapped in a deathly pall,
    The city beside the sea.

He stood by the couch of rich and poor,
   Through weary night and day,
Watching the spark go out in the dark,
And cruel death come, stiff and stark,
   And fasten upon the clay:
And he thought of the twilight when the stars
   Grew golden in the sky;
When never a word his lips had stirred
   Save "Kiss me," and "Good by."

III.

Hither and thither the death carts sped,
   And the city was wan with woe;
For never a spot had death forgot,
And crape hung down from castle and cot,
   And the waving wind breathed low.
Fair were the stars and bright the dew,
   But how could the people know!
For the men were cowed and the women were bowed,
Fearing to comfort each other aloud,
And the moonlight hung like a saffron shroud
   On the prostrate earth below.

*   *   *   *   *

IV.

She sat in her mountain home afar,
    And sad was her heart in its pain;
For the summer was fled, and the blossoms were dead,
And the spirit-winds, tossing the broken leaves, said,
    "He will not come back again."
And she thought of the twilight when the stars
    Grew golden in the sky,
When never a word his pale lips stirred
    Save "Kiss me," and "Good by."

V.

She pined in her dreary mountain home,
    For the wintry sky was gray;
And her heart beat low as the sifting snow
Fell on the hills and the bottoms below,
And feeling her sad heart wed to woe,
    She knelt her down to pray.
And she prayed: "If God be a merciful God,
    In pity look down on me!
And save *him* from harms, to these empty arms,
    In the city beside the sea."

She lifted her face from the dust—"Thank God!"
    And she rushed to her darling's breast;
For the saffron king, on his fatal wing,
Had claimed him not as an offering,
And she clung to him close, like some tenderest thing,
    And sobbed herself to rest.

VI.

And so while the snow-flakes fluttered down,
    Like blanched buds from the sky,
Full many a word his rich lips stirred,
And "Kiss me, sweetheart," oft was heard,
    But never again "Good by."

THE BLOSSOM AND THE BREEZE.

I.

THERE was a blossom fairer far
    Than lilies are,
And sweeter than the sweetest rose
    That overflows
With fragrant sighs beneath the skies,
    To twilight's glorious star.

II.

And to this blossom, pure and bright,
    One glowing night,
A breeze from haunts of summer seas
    And orange-trees,
By some fierce spell, no tongue may tell,
    Was guided in his flight.

III.

The fond wind from his waving plumes
   Shook thick perfumes,
And sighed as sadly as the pale
   And spectral gale,
Whose melancholy pinions trail
   O'er long-forgotten tombs.

IV.

Then, on the cradle of his breast,
   He rocked to rest
The wondrous glory of the flower,
   That blissful hour,
And softly sung with honeyed tongue
   To her he loved the best.

V.

O, tender was the truth, and true,
   Between the two,
When to her lover's wooing arms,
   Her blushing charms,
The blossom bright, that starry night,
   So passionately threw.

VI.

But suddenly a shadow stole
  Across the soul
Of blossom and of breeze—a shape
  With wings of crape,
That urged its flight athwart the night
  From out the frozen pole.

VII.

Then from the blossom's cheek the red
  In terror fled,
While silently about her charms
  The ghostly arms
Wove out of ice, in strange device,
  A shroud—for she was dead.

VIII.

And then the sad wind strewed the flowers,
  Through night's long hours,
With bootless tears; and in the fir
  He mourned for her
With all those sweet appeals that stir
  These human hearts of ours.

IX.

But still unto the wind's sad wing
   Sweet odors cling—
Fond waftures from life's faded bloom,
   The soul's perfume ;
And evermore the twilights bring
   The breeze unto the tomb.

BABY'S PRAYER.

THE mute white snow-flakes drifted
 From a dim and dusky sky,
And my darling's eyes were lifted
 From a sweet face, soft and shy,
As the firelight shone and shifted,
 And the Christmas-tide drew nigh.

She sat at my feet in silence,
 And I knew some deep request
Like a prayer was hung on her silent tongue,
 That a fond hope was suppressed,
That a song in the soul was still unsung,
 Like a tune in a dreamer's breast.

Then I smoothed her fluffy tresses
 And sought for the hidden cause,
And said, "What is it oppresses
 My child?" Then, after a pause,

She said, "Please, mamma, I duesses
    I'll wite to dood Santa Claus!"

So she sat in the glow of the firelight,
    With paper and ink and pen,
And wrote : "I pray that Santa Claus may
    Bring candy and nuts agen ;
But he mustn't fordet a nice tea-set,
    For Desus Christ's sake, amen."

And when on the fateful morning
    The stocking hung huge and fair,
With fat sides swelling as cunningly telling
    The treasures in ambush there,
She cried in delight, all crimson and white,
And beautiful after the balm of the night,
    "O mamma, he answered my prayer !"

And I pray that the heavenly Giver,
    The giver of gifts divine,
May shelter from harm with his mighty arm
    This opening bud of mine,
And take it to rest on his gentle breast
    When loosed from its earthly vine.

LEGEND OF THE KISSIMMEE.

I.

FULL many a long, long year ago,
  In the land of sighing pines,
Where the daintiest blossoms forever blow,
And the breath of the breeze is as sweetly low
  As a love-song in the vines,

II.

A dark-eyed Indian maid abode,
  With a heart still proudly free,
For the hand of fate had opened the gate
Which darkens the years, and bade her wait,
  And she bowed to the mystery.

112

III.

Full many a dusky suitor came
  And wooed in the dewy hours ;
But her virgin breast was still unpressed
When she threw her olive charms to rest
  On her fragrant couch of flowers.

IV.

And then, one warm and languorous eve,
  With a new and strange delight,
She heard a crush of the underbrush,
And her heart beat audibly in the hush
  Of the still and starry night ;

V.

For out of the shadows strode a youth
  With a golden cloud of hair,
And a sweet blue eye, like an April sky,
Over which the clouds like shadows fly
  To leave it still more fair.

VI.

The star-rays fell in a storm of light,
　　And the man and the maid were dumb;
But the girl's great eyes shone under the skies
With a luminous, glad, and soft surprise,
　　For she felt that her fate had come.

VII.

And when from the stranger's rose-red lips
　　A quaint sweet murmur fell,
She knew what it meant by the thrill it sent
To her longing heart—and she was content
　　To look what she could not tell.

VIII.

And the nut-brown arms reached out and up,
　　With a touching and tender grace,
And she hung at rest on her idol's breast
As her passionate heart was fondly pressed
　　In the fold of his sweet embrace.

*　　　　*　　　　*　　　　*　　　　*

IX.

Full many a moon had waxed and waned,
    And the youth with the golden hair
Still murmured of love to his wildwood dove,
While blossoms rained down from the bowers above
    And gladdened the glowing air.

X.

And the loved and loving Indian maid
    In her mate's strange language cooed,
But its dreariest note in her golden throat
From a hidden harp-string seemed to float
    In the flowery solitude.

XI.

One warm October afternoon
    This youth of the maiden's heart,
With bow in hand, by the silver sand
Of a river which coursed through that fair land,
    Was aiming his deadly dart.

XII.

For his ear had caught the snap of a twig
　　'Neath the weight of a cautious tread,
And the sudden sway of a myrtle spray
Unveiled a glimpse of his lurking prey
　　In its fresh and flowery bed.

XIII.

A twang of the bow-string, and the flash
　　And flight of the cruel dart,
And the maiden lay in the shadows gray,
Sighing her true young soul away
　　On her husband's broken heart.

XIV.

She told the tale of her loneliness,
　　And her quest by the river's brink
For the form so fair, with its golden hair,
For she knew that his step would tarry there
　　Till the deer came down to drink.

XV.

And then as her life was drifting out
    To the weird and waveless sea,
With a queenly grace she swept the trace
Of a tear from her darling's livid face,
    And said, " Sweet love, kissa me ! "

XVI.

And so with that sad and pure embrace
    On her quivering lips impressed,
Her life's young flower from its earthly bower
Was caught to the stars in the twilight hour,
    And laid upon mercy's breast.

*   *   *   *   *

XVII.

'Twas many a long, long year ago,
    But the Indian maid's request
Shall ever abide the name of the tide
Upon whose tropical bank she died,
    And where her ashes rest.

PAWNING THE PETTICOAT.

I.

YES, stranger, those was high old times,
    And seein' as how it's you,
I'll mention the job we worked on Bob
    In eighteen fifty-two.
Well, yes; if you think a previous drink
    Wud hurry the story through.

II.

You see this Bob was a tenderfoot,
    But he had onusule eyes
That showed the stuff ter weaken a rough,
    An' stands in the place of size;
So the boys agreed that he wouldn't bluff,
    Which no one yet denies.

III.

Well, stranger, arter a lengthy spell,
　　Which I am proud ter say,
Bob struck it rich with a sluicin' ditch
　　An' tuk out thundering pay,
Then treated the town, from the bar-keep down,
　　An' left on the follerin' day.

IV.

Some six or eight months arterwards,
　　When the boys was on a spree,
A-slingin' the dust in the way the wust
　　Perhaps that ever I see,
Ole Flowery Pete riz up on his feet
　　An' fired a wink at me.

V.

An' layin' his holt on my shoulder, so,
　　A-seekin' the natur'l plumb,
He drug me up ter the soshil cup
　　(Containin' the best of rum),
An' takin' a most almighty dost,
　　Remarked, " Miss Bob has come!"

VI.

Ag'in?—say, stranger, I'm not dry,
    Onless—well, gimme a sweet;
Or what do you think of the soshil drink
    I took with Flowery Pete?
Jest suits? That's me! so here we be,
    An' may we ofting meet.

VII.

I circled around, you may believe,
    A-scatterin' wide the news;
A-tellin' the boys ter quit the'r noise,
    An' gatherin' diffrunt views;
An' it was agreed that the gal Pete seed
    Was purty as dancin' shoes.

VIII.

But women had never come before,
    An' Bob had shook the gang;
So the Jedge and me talked privatelee,
    While Pete an' the fellers sang;
But we couldn't decide what ter do with the bride
    In case it was a hang.

IX.

It wasn't the gal so much, you know,
    We sorter give in ter that,
But women will bring sich an endless string
    Of parsons, ter pass the hat;
So me an' the Jedge was clean on edge,
    Like the tail of a tousled cat.

X.

We couldn't agree, the Jedge an' me,
    So we went for a soshil glass,
An' it helped me some, fur an idee come
    I didn't allow ter pass,
So I told the boys ter quit the'r noise
    An' form in a judgment class.

XI.

An' then we helt a kinder court,
    An' the case was fairly tried—
Fur the Jedge an' me was sober, you see
    (Which never has been denied),
An' we finerly said, that alive or dead,
    The boys should see the bride.

XII.

An' that ain't all—the court an' me
    Composed the plaintive's fine,
A mild invite, in words perlite,
    Fur Bob ter furnish the wine;
Then Flowery Pete waltzed inter the street
    An' formed us in a line.

XIII.

The boys was very quiet like,
    But walked in ways amazin',
An' the Jedge an' me was constantlee
    Kept wonderin' an' a-gazin';
Fur I must say them boys that day
    Showed *terrible* good raisin'.

XIV.

We halted at the cabin gate,
    An' the Jedge an' me went in,
An' we found the lass at her lookin'-glass
    A-fixin' a diamon' pin:
An' the Jedge was red all over his head
    A-wonderin' whar ter begin.

XV.

An' I never see a purtier face
    Than I see thar an' then,
Fur her doe-like eyes was a fine surprise
    At the mob of drunken men;
So the Jedge an' me says soothinlee,
    "Thar's only a hundred an' ten!"

XVI.

Then we perlitely ast fur Bob,
    But he was at the mine;
So we bowed as low as our heads wud go,
    An' j'ined the staggerin' line;
But the boys was as full as a tick on a bull,
    An' howled fur a tank of wine.

XVII.

Then Pete stepped forth an' spoke a piece,
    An', stranger, you'd a died!
He said as Bob was off at his job,
    Supposin' we pawned the bride,
An' Bob's ole mar' a-standin' thar
    Wud give 'er a way-up ride.

XVIII.

I don't know how it happened next,
    But somehow Flowery Pete
Come out with the bride, rigged up fur a ride,
    An' lookin' tremenjous sweet;
An' her cheeks was red—so the fellers said—
    An' tender enough ter eat.

XIX.

An' so we fetched Miss Bob ter the bar,
    An' read what we had wrote,
When Pete, like a fool, clomb up on a stool
    An' called for a risin' vote!
But we shet him up with a soshil cup
    An' mortgaged the petticoat.

XX.

Another, stranger? Well, I will,
    If this makes—yes, makes two:
I'll take the same, which I need not name,
    A drop of the soshil dew;
An' here's success ter yer little game,
    An' health an' wealth ter you.

XXI.

Well, that's about the way it was,
 An' the boys got squar'ly blind;
But the Jedge an' me kept sober ter see
 How Bob wud show his mind;
But he paid the bill with a right good-will,
An' galloped the mar' back down the hill,
 A-packin' his wife behind.

XXII.

An' sence that time Miss Bob has been
 The purtiest gal that grows,
Fur the boys confess she ain't no less
 'Than a saint in female close—
Which same ter deny is a weepin' eye,
 An' the bloodiest sort of nose.

XXIII.

Well, good by, stranger: call ag'in;
 An' are you travelin' fur?
It's no more good in Cottonwood,
 An' the times ain't got no stir—
Say! up the street—that's Flowery Pete,
 A-walkin' along o' *her.*

OREGON SUE.

A Legend of '53.

I.

WELL, stranger, here you are ag'in;
  Now take a smile with me:
Jest kind of light, an' bide all night,
  For board an' bed is free—
Not countin' a yarn you'd like ter l'arn—
  Come in! What shall it be?

II.

The same? Now that is soshil like,
  So here's a-lookin' ter you;
An' here's ter the wife—what! dern my life
  If I ain't heard you'd two!
Well, here's may you find a lass ter your mind,
  A lovin' one, an' a true.

III.

Jest set down while I stir the fire
　　An' tumble the nag some hay,
For you an' the brute is in cahoot
　　A-honorin' me this day:
So freeze ter a seat an' toast your feet—
　　I won't be gone ter stay.

*　　　　*　　　　*　　　　*　　　　*

IV.

The yarn? Well, back in 'fifty-three
　　The wimmen was raly few,
So Flowery Pete got frightful sweet
　　On a Injin gal he knew;
An' I seldom see two folks agree
　　Like him an' Oregon Sue.

V.

An' this I say, that an ugly mug
　　Belongs ter the Injin race,
But Oregon Sue was white cl'ar through
　　In spite of her yaller face,
An' her close was clean as ever I seen
　　In the most respectful place.

VI.

So the Jedge an' me, accordin'lee,
    Without a blot or flaw,
Drawed up a writ a-statin' it
    That Pete could take the squaw ;
An' the boys all signed, fur ter make it bind,
    Providin' it come ter law.

VII.

An' arter the sarvice Pete an' Sue
    Remained thar, side by side,
For well they knew the entire crew
    Was waitin' ter kiss the bride ;
An' when it was done, an' Pete took one,
    She fell on his neck an' cried.

VIII.

It wasn't the thing, perhaps, ter do,
    But the boys agreed with me,
That she went ter rest on her pardner's breast,
    The sweetest that ever we see—
A-lookin', we said, like a rosebud red,
    A-twinin' around a tree.

IX.

An', strange as it sounds, the last man thar
    Was actin' the plainest lie,
Ter make it appear it wasn't a tear
    A-gatherin' in his eye;
But the Jedge an' me could certingly see
    Thar wasn't a dern one dry.

X.

An' thinkin' the gal was lonesome like,
    With nothin' but men in sight,
We straggled away with nothin' ter say,
    An' dodged about in the night;
An' my partin' view was Oregon Sue
    A-huggin' him clost an' tight.

XI.

Well, in them days the Injun tribes
    Was buckin' in ways severe;
An' signal-lights shone out o' nights
    On the mountings, fur and near;
But Flowery's bride bein' on our side,
    We didn't have much ter fear.

XII.

One night she seen the suddent flash
    Of a green, onusule star,
An' she said it meant that the tribes was bent
    On liftin' the miners' ha'r—
An' you may believe, which I won't deceive,
    They come—an' they found us *thar!*

XIII.

We left Miss Bob an' Oregon Sue
    With a guard drawed out ter stay,
Then inter the shade that the mountings made
    We silently stole away,
As willin'—as glad—ter fight by night
    As ever we was by day.

XIV.

But Sue got out and dodged the guard,
    An' never lost sight of Pete ;
An' the boys all say she blazed away
    In a style it was hard ter beat ;
An' Pete was as proud as a tipsy crowd
    A-packin' her down the street.

XV.

The signal-fires still blazed around,
    But the imps was monstrous shy,
For well they knew that Oregon Sue
    Could sleep with an open eye;
An' venturin' out was gitten about
    The same thing as ter die.

XVI.

So winter come. 'Twas Christmas eve—
    That's right! Don't wait for me;
You want it hot? As well as not—
    That's Flowery ter a T,
An' Oregon Sue could mix a stew
    The touchin'est ever I see.

XVII.

Well, stranger, snow was driftin' fast,
    In flakes so wide acrost
That Flowery Pete a-crossin' the street
    Come dern nigh gitten lost;
But we warmed him up with a soshil cup,
    An' laughed at the fallin' frost.

XVIII.

An' airly Christmas day, when we
    Was pilotin' Pete ter bed,
Thar wasn't a stick nor stone nor brick
    Ter kiver his curly head;
An' under the snow, by a broken bow,
    The pride of his life lay dead.

XIX.

We planted her under an old oak tree,
    A-keepin' the fact in mind,
That lettin' the bark be ever so dark,
    A white heart hides behind;
An' Oregon Sue had a soul as true
    As the fairest of womankind.

DEAD MAN'S BAR.

I.

THEY used ter call this Dead Man's Bar,
    And if you wish the why,
I happen ter know how come it so
    (Which no one will deny);
For I worked here then, with a gang of men,
    In the claim you're settin' by.

II.

One day while techin' off a blast,
    With somethin' else in mind,
A man was blowed in a way we knowed
    Wud finerly make him blind ;
So we sent him East with a rattlin' beast,
    An' the best guide we could find.

133

III.

The guide, his name was Portagee Joe,
    A yallerish-lookin' case,
With here an' thar a stragglin' ha'r
    A-hangin' in keerless grace,
But his eyes was keen as ever I seen
    In a livin' human's face.

IV.

The boys all come ter the startin' out,
    An' we sent 'm off in style,
Full up ter the chin with the best of gin,
    An' bottles for arter a while;
An' the bags of dust, from last to fust,
    Was a most respectful pile.

V.

We stood right whar we're settin' now,
    An' watched 'm climb the trail,
An' the last we heard was a grateful word
    In the blind man's partin' hail;
So I turned away with my heart that day
    As big as a yearlin' whale.

VI.

We kinder knocked off work that day,
　　Because the boys all said
That goin' away ter the East to stay
　　Was somethin' like goin' dead;
So we writ a pome on the joys of home,
　　Which the drunken bar-keep read.

VII.

Next day a rumer come ter camp,
　　That wasn't believed by me,
Which said that Joe was seed ter go
　　A-boatin'—which might be—
But it was shown he was alone,
　　An' paddlin' for the sea.

VIII.

That day we found the blind man, dead,
　　With his rattlin' beast clost by,
An' the boys all felt like the'r hearts wud melt
　　(Not bein' the gang ter cry),
For they couldn't unsay that goin' away
　　Was pretty much like ter die.

IX.

We buried him by that biggest fir,
    But we didn't turn on no pray'r,
For we all agreed that he had no need
    Of help that a man could spar';
An' we put it down that he'd git his crown,
    If heaven was on the squar'.

X.

Well, Portagee Joe had stole a boat,
    For the trail he knowed full well
Wud give us a clew we'd foller cl'ar through
    Ter Afriky or ter hell ;
So he took the boat, a-hopin' ter float,
    Whar nothin' was left ter tell.

XI.

But show me a craft in the univarse
    Can paddle the Klamath through,
For the shoals an' rocks etarnally knocks
    The best of 'm black an' blue ;
An' arter a while—I'll give 'm a mile—
    The stoutest is broke in two.

XII.

So Joe an' the gin an' the dust went down,
    But the boat was washed ashore,
The sorriest wreck, I do expeck,
    That ever was seed before ;
But the onery guide slunk under the tide,
    And never come up no more.

XIII.

Well, well ! It's many a good long year
    Sence plantin' the blind one thar ;
But my stiff'nin' j'ints is the only p'ints
    (An' the whit'nin' of my ha'r)
That makes me know how long ago
    I mined on Dead Man's Bar.

THE GROWL OF THE GOLD-DIGGER.

I.

I AIN'T no hand ter kick or buck
　　Agin a losin' run of luck,
　　　　Not even if I'm busted ;
But raly, if I was a saint
(Which you may rightly judge I ain't
　　　　With being scripter rusted),
I couldn't help from speakin' out,
An' may be cussin, too, about
　　　　The way that I am wusted.

II.

I don't complain of little pay,
Which nat'rally declines away
　　　　In ways sometimes expected ;

But when the children on the claims
Is named the most jaw-breakin' names
   It's time that I objected.
For now we've got, ter all intents,
More kernels, kings, and presidents
   Than ever was elected.

III.

Thar's Greasy Jake on Chiny Flat
Has named his last forthcomin' brat
   Mahony Adams Linkum,
An' Josh has named his youngest gal
Miss Roseoler Balmoral
   Elizerbelly Pinkum,
When neither one ain't worth the lead,
Much less the rope, when all is said,
   That it wud take ter sink 'm.

IV.

Thar's Shote, a squaw-man, with a gang
Of young uns growin' up ter hang
   Onless they greatly alter;

For Alfred Byron Marmaduke,
An' Simon Revelations Luke,
      Is sp'ilin' for the halter ;
An' so is Stonewall Moses Lee,
An' Judus Guiteau Saducee
      Pythagoras Gibralter.

V.

Virginny Cleopatrer Rose
An' Luna Gracie Adipose
      Is gals upon the marry ;
But all the boys has said ter Shote
They jedged the'r fortunes couldn't float
      With so much style ter carry ;
Still Shote he called the final one
Posthumous Spiral Rubicon
      Integumental Harry.

VI.

Olfactory Snipe has eight or ten,
For instance : Ebenezer Ben
      Sir Walter Homer Tanner,

Helena Shakspere Simplified,
Pelucid Astor Ingleside
        Indigenous Bandanner,
Eructible Rebecker Ruth,
An' likewise Boberlink Forsooth
        Imprimis Susquehanner.

VII.

Thar's David Oleander Grant
(Whose eyes is most tremenjous slant
        An' legs is bowed amazin'—
An' I must say my mind ain't fixed
On which is most infernal mixed,
        His walkin' or his gazin') ;
An' thar's his sister Ivanhoe
Saint Agnis, which I bet ter know
        More deviltry than raisin'.

VIII.

Thar's Revrund Barnum Beechers Toe,
A twin ter Ikabod Defoe
        Sartoris Salamander ;

An' Medieval Tildun Blaine
(Another twin—ter Ponchertraine
   Polaris Alexander);
An' last, not least, is Eglantine
Ginevrer Donna Ginuine
   Miss Burdett Couts Mirander.

IX.

I've had the measles, rheumatiz,
An' all the wust of ills thar is,
   But they was quite a frolic—
Was recreations of delight,
An' pleasanter a dogon sight
   Than names so dierbolic;
For Grundy Colfax Omnibus
Sut Lovingood upsets me wuss
   Than cramps assistin' colic.

X.

My arms and legs was frequent broke,
Which no one heard a cuss word spoke
   Though constant recommended;

But thar's a p'int whar human grit
Gits weakened, like a bow when it
   Is kept eternal bended ;
An' so as kickin' ain't no use,
It's rulable to cut aloose
   As latterly intended.

XI.

I principally hate ter growl,
But durn my picter for an owl
   If this ain't overdoin' !
I'd ruther, as a constant thing,
Set down upon a hornit's sting,
   Or fight a hungry bruin,
Than everlastin'ly ter hear
Them titles ringin' in my ear,
   Amountin' ter blue ruin.

XII.

I come out here in 'forty-nine,
But now I'm ready to resign
   An' shake all ol' connections.

I want to find some blessid spot
Whar children ain't—at least is not
      Beholden to elections
An' sich for names that, ciphered out,
Wud kiver nigh onter about
      A mile in all directions.

SONG OF THE KLAMATH.

I.

A MERRY and mad and terrible stream,
   That dashes and gleams and gloats
O'er dead men's bones and golden stones,
   And the wreck of a thousand boats.
O'er the strangled tones and muffled moans
   Of a throng of silent throats.

II.

Ay, terrible, merry, and mad they say,
   Though I revel and roll in smiles;
But the human race with its pallid face
Will hurry away from my dread embrace
   As I dance through the mountain aisles.

III.

And well may they fear this timorous tribe,
    For I fancy a singular toll,
And oft as I can from my enemy, man,
    I snatch a reluctant soul.

IV.

Then madly I toy with the pitiful clay
    Which struggled and gasped and died,
And into his arms all my treasure of charms
    I cast like a newly made bride.

V.

I kiss the warm glory of hair from his brow,
    And cradle him on my breast ;
But his lips are as mute as a stringless lute,
And I know that it is but Dead Sea fruit
    My circling arms have pressed.

VI.

Then over the rapids and rocks away
    I rush with my rigid prize,
And anchor him deep in an icy sleep,
While friends make search and kindred weep,
    And a maiden sobs and sighs.

VII.

And finally swollen, bruised, and black,
    I lift him up on a wave,
And heave him aside—this mother's pride—
With nothing left in the world beside
    A coffin and a grave.

VIII.

Ay, terrible, merry, and mad am I
    When some rude wall intrudes
His bulwark gray, as though to say
He questioned my queenly right of way
    Through the mountain solitudes.

IX.

I flaunt my crest in the face of the sky,
　　And charge with a mighty shriek,
And the looming rock gives way to the shock,
While echoes fly like birds in a flock
　　From many a polar peak.

X.

Then over the grinding mass I leap
　　With my flossy hair outflung,
And the wind sweeps down to brighten a crown
From the wall of granite, broken and brown,
　　By these fierce fingers wrung.

XI.

Then on and on, with a rush and roar
　　And a shout of victory !
With a mocking wail to the howling gale,
And a hiss to the mortals stricken pale,
　　And mute with awe of me ;
Forever on to the tender hail
　　Of my love in the solemn sea.

XII.

A merry and mad and terrible stream
　　Through a Christian land to flow,
With dimples that ride on its scintillant tide,
To lure the unwary, as well as to hide
　　Its treacherous undertow.

XIII.

Be it so ; but still, as the years glide by,
　　I shall gather my ghostly toll ;
For I hate the face of the human race,
　　And the slavery of the soul.

"TRANQUILLA."

A GROVE of oaks whose green arms interwoven
Athwart the grassy lawn their umbrage throw;
Imperial plumes and clumps of verdure, cloven
By silver missiles from the moon's bright bow,
While symphonies, as of some rapt Beethoven,
From out the bascage tremble, sweet and low,
And like a palace in a veil of foam,
Amidst the twilight rises childhood's home.

I wander back through avenues of madness,
Through dews of disappointment and regret;
Through dusky aisles where broods a sweet-eyed sadness
Among the dreams she cannot all forget;
And out into the phantom realm of gladness
And afterglow of suns forever set,
Where memory-buds in silent beauty blow
Among the evergreens of long ago.

How mightily the Chattahoochee rushes
 With wondrous contributions to the sea !
How tenderly night's dim and distant hushes
 The mocking-bird invades with melody !
While virgin roses strew the earth with blushes
 And jasmines cast their curls from every tree !
For in a spell I fondly muse and float
Within the years, the cherished, the remote.

Above me Kennesaw is grandly looming,
 A stately pillar in a billowed plain,
The purple of his princely shadow glooming
 The golden armor of the serried grain,
While on his brow the rose of sunset blooming
 Along the landscape sifts a ruby rain,
And one ray-blossom, like a blessing, falls
Upon Tranquilla's oak-embowered walls.

I stand within my chamber, at whose casement
 A deep-hued poplar all his glory swings,
While here and there, up-creeping from the basement,
 An ivy leaf its tender message brings—

A leaf, like love, that overlooks displacement,
    And still for coldness but the closer clings—
And then I sigh that thus its heart hath grown
Like mine about an unresponsive stone.

I stand and muse on each familiar token
    That hangs before me eloquent and mute,
Renewing links in life that time hath broken,
    Out-calling olden chords from passion's lute,
And resurrecting vows more looked than spoken,
    Fair promise-buds that bore no happy fruit;—
I stand and muse, then sadly, one and all,
I turn their patient faces to the wall.

And then a silver bell's soft note comes stealing
    Along the darkness wooing unto prayer,
And in the dear and sacred circle kneeling
    I lose the sinking consciousness of care,
And only know that love, and faith, and feeling,
    And constancy are all united there;
While in the world but specters we pursue,
And reaching out for roses, gather rue.

SHADOWS OF DAWN.

TO DELL.

I.

WANDERING in the gloaming, precious,
Under all the stars that mesh us
In their toils of light,
Wish I fondly thou wert folden
To my heart as in the olden,
Golden days, to-night.

II.

Listening to the streams that darkle
Down the mountain-ribs, and sparkle
With the gems they bear,
Dream I that in every floated
Murmur from the silver-throated
Ripples, thou art near.

155

III.

Yet 'tis all a sweet illusion,
But a sunbeam's swift intrusion
  On a grated cell ;
Merely incense floated over
Cliff and canyon from the clover
  In a distant dell.

IV.

So, beside the singing stream, I
Linger, dreaming still the dream I
  Dreamt in days gone by ;—
Idly dream till morning edges
With a rosy rim the ledges
  Of the dappled sky.

V.

Ah, the sweet ! and ah, the bitter !
Ah ! the mingled gloom and glitter
  In the woof of years !
Mountain streams moan disappointment,
And a-weary hope no ointment
  Yields my heart but tears.

TO A FALSE CHARMER.

LOVED I thee? Ah! 'twas a fleeting
       Fancy that beset my mind ;
For I find myself repeating,
Since my heart is calmly beating,
       "Coldness was but being kind."

Still, the gentle thoughts I bore thee
       Are abandoned with regret :
And in dreams I still adore thee,
Still as foolishly implore thee,
       Ne'er my passion to forget.

Castles had I built—but broken
       Is the charm which made them fair,
And there bides no sign nor token
Of our love-tale, looked or spoken,
       With its vows of empty air.

Deem not that I would upbraid thee,
 For thou wert to me as just
As the mold of nature made thee;
As the fickle thought that swayed thee
 As a woman to her trust!

FANCIES IN THE FIRE.

I SIT and look into the coals; they seem
    To languish lazily the while I dream
And ponder as the colored gases rise
Inflamed before me; but my poring eyes
Can scarce be said to truly recognize
    The rosy conflagration, for each warm,
Ephemeral expression as it flies
    Athwart the furnace is a face, a form,
A picture, and each fleeting jet of flame
    Some sweetest thought suggests. In idleness
I thus commune with memory till each same
    Familiar incident agone doth press
    Its tender presence. Ah! I would confess
That in this hushed inclosure of the mind
A thousand fragrant thoughts and things I find
Among the shadows.

As into the waves
The diver headlong plunges, and from graves
With jewels from the mermaids' golden hair
Encrusted plucks his booty scattered there,
So I into the past, by silence led,
Still dreaming, wander, and I gather red

And incense-laden memories that grow
Above the tombs within the gloaming. Green
The grasses are along the path I know
So well, and sunny-bosomed doves between
The intervals of silence coo, as through
The riven cloud-rack falls a gleam of blue
In April. But forever vanished now
The days that have been, save within the pale
Which Love hath thrown around her treasures. Thou
Hast known the exercise of soul, and how
Love's arms entwine the thoughts that do but sail
Along the rim of recollection. So
My heart; but dearer far than all I know
A thought, a fairy thought, as clean as snow,
And warm as summer twilight when the dew
Hath scarce begun to gather; and to you
This gentle thought its sweet existence owes;
I see a bright fair face which ever grows

By gazing on't more fair. I see bright eyes
Look into mine, as from the open skies
The stars shine on the sea, diffusing light
Along the waste of waters and the night;
I see—since 'tis a picture—little feet
    Half hidden, half disclosed, that barely reach
The carpet; and bright cheeks as fresh and sweet
    As tinted morning-glories, while on each
Of two rich lips a crimson glory dwells.
I feel a timid hand in mine;—that tells
The story! O, the brown hair on the brow!
The yearning, soulful gaze! To heaven I vow
My little one—and thee, that at thy shrine
    Henceforth I worship. Years and years have flown
    Since first we met, but now with thought alone
My mute companion, every look of thine
Comes drifting to me from the silent sea,
And in my heart I feel, I know, that we
    Have to each other more than dearly grown;
And in the picture-coals rise ghosts of thee,
Whose sad eyes look a soft "Come back to me."
Would that I might! If strength of love could bear
The burden of a feather in the air,

My soul's devotion would so far exceed
The love of men that, like a bird, I'd speed
　　Rejoicing to thy feet.

　　　　　　　　The hours glide by,
The bells throb out eleven, and as die
The trembling intonations, and the wind
Sighs through the trees, I still can find
　　A sympathetic sadness in the tone —
A plaintiveness to which my weary mind
　　Can turn, and feel, though lonely, less alone.

MY SWEETHEART.

I HAVE a sweetheart fair to see,
    With hair as brightly brown
As ever curled in Paradise
    About an angel's crown.

Her lips are dewy with delights,
    And kissed with crimson hue;
And in her eyes are starry skies
    With love-stars glowing through.

And she hath lily hands, I ween,
    With soft and peachy palms,
And, like her lips, her finger tips
    Are charged with magic balms.

And merry dancing feet hath she
That dimple all the lawn,
When sunrise hurls his golden curls
Unto the blushing dawn.

The pink and pearly-throated shell,
Which loves the summer sea,
No music sighs but that she hies
To murmur it to me.

And in this wide old wondrous world
Our hearts shall still entwine,
Until the ivy's flag is furled
Above her dust and mine.

HER NAME.

I HAVE a friend. Her name? Hard by the rill
    Between the green flags coursing, birds are singing
And caroling her name. The stream which still
    Upon its happy little breast is bringing
Sweet freights of broken blossoms from the hill
    Whereon the wild-flowers congregate, can tell
As well as I. The night wind in the roses
    Whose fairy wings beat fragrance from the bell
Of nodding blossom which at even closes
    And folds its curtains, whispers, as it flies,
The secret of her name.

                    Hast thou not heard
A moaning in the pines, whose harps are stirred
    By spirit fingers? Hast thou, when the skies
    Are gloamy, and the soulful twilight dies

Away into a starry silence, caught
    Some soft, delicious symphony of song
    Unborn of earth, which sweeps and swells along
The purple atmosphere? — a music fraught
With hints of summer seas, and droning shells,
And sweetest violets in dewy dells?
These breathe her winsome name ; — the very rain
Which patters on the furrowed window-pane
Repeats the soft refrain — and yet again,
As though by fond reiterance to press
A dim suspicion of the loveliness
The words imply. Ask of the burnished dove,
In sunny dingles murmuring her love,
The tender story which I may not tell,
The name which violets and roses spell
In perfume — which the angels in my dreams
Unto each other whisper — which the streams,
O'erhung with tangled blossoms coyly trace
With mocking waves that write but to erase.
Ask of the twilight's purple, morning's gold,
But ask not me this fond name to unfold.

NEMESIS.

I CANNOT sleep to-night; a shadow dwells
Upon the threshold of my chamber door;
A ghostly Presence stalks across the floor
In silence, and I feel it sweeping o'er
My life; while audibly the midnight swells
From bells that hang in churchyards, and from bells
In belfries everywhere.

            I cannot sleep;
I hear the rags of gaunt Ill-fortune sweep
Along the isolation of my room,
And feel the specter in the heavy gloom
Infolding me. The stars in one huge shroud
Are buried; and the tears from every cloud
Are dripping on my heart. Along the street
The lamplights shed a glamour, but the feet

That hurry through the storm no comfort bring
Unto my solitude. The leathern wing
Of this dark bat which flaps along the wall
Is more my true companion now than all
    The multitude of men. My friends—alas !
I have none now—had never ! and I pray
That in this life again I never may,
To kiss the cheek, like Judas, and betray.
    There was a time when hope—that too may pass ;
The butterfly hath turned a creeping thing,
And where was erst a rainbow of a wing
Is now but rottenness.

                I cannot sleep !
A dreadful Absence haunts me, and I keep
Communion with a Curse whose fingers hook
    Upon the veil about the future ; wide
It draws the curtaining, and from the Book
    Wherein is written all that shall betide,
Such dreary passages recites that I,
    To horror still unused, am in despair,
    While prophecies involve the choking air,
And like to evil things on dark wings fly,

And circle over me. I feel the brush
Of spectral pinions beating in the hush
About me, and I shudder, though the air
Is close, and ever and anon the glare
Of lightnings brand the night.

                     O, cruel Fate !
  Why to these lips dost thou unkindly press
Thy bitter chalice? Why this desolate,
    Aweary heart, whose utter loneliness
No love assuages, dost thou still delight
In torturing? Why dost thou, in the night,
With strange creations hem me, and outpour
    Upon my racking brain this grim despair?
Alas! thy bleak wings through my slumbers soar
    Until I even dream that love, so fair,
Is false. There was a maiden from whose eye
    No guile looked out. Her lips were as the rose,
The red, ripe rose, when twilight zephyrs sigh
    In spring-time, and the golden gateways close
Behind the coursers of the sun ; and she
So sweet and bud-like in her purity,
So like a cooing dove, in one mad hour
Enslaved me—and the fragrance of the flower

Still haunts me. Ah ! the fevered dream is flown,
And I abide in wretchedness alone ;
The sport of sad repinings and regrets,
The while my heart all other thought forgets,
And struggling in the chafings of its chains,
But wounds itself, and multiplies its pains.

SONG OF LIFE.

I.

THROB! Throb! Throb!
 'Tis the restless heart's refrain;
The burden sad of the ocean's song,
Sweeping its fretted sands along;
 Tearing the corals and pearls from its caves,
 Lifting them up on its petulant waves,
  And dashing them back again.

II.

 Thrill! Thrill! Thrill!
 And the chalice of bliss runs o'er;
The nestling head on the heaving breast,
Drooping and sinking unto its rest,
 The while impassioned arms entwine,
 Awakening ecstasies divine,
  That ne'er were felt before.

III.

Throb ! Throb ! Throb !
And the watches vigil keep;
The night wind sighs through the cedar's surge,
And Death comes in with the ghostly dirge,
Closing the eyelids over their glass,
And the watchers are mourners, alas and alas !
And the women bow down and weep.

IV.

Thrill ! Thrill ! Thrill !
And the music palpitates,
While happy feet in circles glide,
Like flowers afloat on a dimpled tide,
Careless of where their feet be cast,
so they haply come at last,
Through Pleasure's palace gates.

V.

Throb ! Thrill ! Throb !
O, how the discord swells !
And hope and fear, and smile and tear,
Woven together year by year,
Daylight and darkness, gloom and glow,
Mingled in one weird theme, as though
Of bridal-burial bells.

STILL WILL I HAPPY BE.

I.

WHEN in my fairest dreams
    Visions I see;
Each a reflection seems,
    Loved one, of thee;
For in thine azure eyes,
Love like a jewel lies,
    Shining for me.

II.

And in my bosom, deep
    Cloistered aside,
Pure as a pearl asleep
    Under the tide,
Only thine image reigns;
No other thought remains
    Love to divide.

III.

And there thy vows so true
    Sweetly repose,
Like starry gems of dew,
    Clasped by a rose ;
And how my fond heart reels
With all the bliss it feels,
    Nobody knows.

IV.

And when the roses bloom
    Over my head,
Roofing my lowly tomb,
    Fragrant and red,
Still will I happy be,
For thou shalt come to me,
    Come still, though dead.

THE FATAL PLEDGE.

ALONG the beetling crags and cliffs that bowed
    Their shaggy outline to the chipping tide,
And threw their ghostly shadows, dense and dim,
Across the distance, sighed the summer wind,
And down the aisles of air obliquely swept
The fleecy gold of sunset; far below,
The river, like a spectral mirror, threw
A weird effulgence on the balmy air
Which grew nigrescent momently—the while,
Upon the topmost bowlder, where the last
Rich reach of glory smote the stately trees
And drowsy blossoms, Hattie sat with Hugh.
The twilight gathered, and the purpling scene
Waxed into wild proportions through the haze,
And mountains rose like giant obelisks
Along the near horizon, for the eye
Could trace but wraiths and vagaries.   The stars

At silent intervals stole into place,
Until in troops and cluster-clouds they wheeled
Along the arc of God; and then the flowers
Outwafted dreamy incense to the winds,
And moonlight hung her royal banner out
Above the scene, while far and faint below,
The river sang a lullaby, and rocked
Itself to sleep.

   So Hugh clasped Hattie's hand
And cried: "How long, my darling, wilt thou thus
The crowning of my love delay? Thy tongue
The temper of thine eye doth oft gainsay,
Refuting to my heart the neutral speech
Wherewith thou crucifiest me. Then here,
Where earth is hushed to rest, and where the soul
Throws off the shackles of its destiny,
Give thou to me the love still unconfessed,
Yet ne'er refused! And, Hattie, shouldst thou doubt,
Then gauge my fierce affection to thy choice!
Bid me from this bare battlement to plunge
Into the stream which kisses as it cuffs
The naked rocks that hem it!—and if I
Shouldst falter in thine order's execution,

Then doom me, Hattie, with a cold reply,
And send me, groping, in the world to die."
The moon hung pale athwart the eastern verge
As though to dip behind the purple screen
Whence she but now had risen. Not a sound,
No stir, save ever and anon the splash
Of multitudes of restless waters.

                       Then
The maiden said : " My hand is fettered, Hugh ;
My heart was always thine—beats still for thee !"

*   *   *   *   *

We may not follow tender word and deed—
Sweet kisses rained on trembling ruby lips,
And fond avowals bursting from the heart
Like blossoms in the tropics! They agreed
According to their worship, and the stars
Looked down and smiled. Then he: "Take thou
      this ring
In token of my faith. In giving it,
I pledge my sacred troth to love but thee."
She took the stone-crowned circlet from his hand,
And drawing from her finger fair a gem,

Gave it to him, and said: "And this to thee
In earnest of my love ; and it shall rest
With thee, a pledge that I am only thine."
She held it forth to him, and as he reached
To clasp the precious gift, it fell, and flashed
Adown the arching height. There, on a twig,
The rayful stone in oscillation hung,
Refracting Luna's crescent argency
Into a fan of beams—a seeming sphere
Of flame invisibly suspended ; or
A fallen star, which wandering down through space
Had poised itself mysteriously bright
Within the dripping concave of the rocks.
"Wait till I get it, Hattie!" Hugh exclaimed,
As down the grim escarpment of the hill
He frantically sprung. Beneath his feet
The moonlit rocks were traitors, bounding down
Into the dim abyss, when trod upon,
With laughter as of scorn. Still Hugh strove on,
From danger into peril, till his hand
Was reaching out to seize the truant pledge.
Then Hattie, from the parapet looked down
And saw her lover stretching forth to clasp
The ring. She saw him free it from the spray,

And heard him shout: "Now, Hattie, thou art mine!"
Then as her eager eyes were on him bent,
She saw him totter in the ghostly light
And grasp the twig on which the gem had shone.
She gazed with icy horror on his face,
Turned upward in a marble pallor.   Then
With one proud hand he held the diamond up,
The fatal diamond, crying, "Thou art mine!"
And so the frail twig parted, and adown
The sullen eminence the lover wheeled.
"Forever thine!" upon the cliff was heard,
And whitely through the night a dress of snow
Was fluttering!—a double splash—a hush—
A thousand circles widening on the stream—
A deeper silence!—and the stars looked down
And kissed the dew-tears weeping Night had shed.

BELLE.

HER eyes are blue, her voice is song,
    Her hair is silken, brown and long—
        O, she is passing fair !
And when she smiles, a sunny glow
    Across each feature flies,
    Like some rare beam that hies
In winter to a drift of snow,
    And flushing one bright moment, dies
        In splendor there.

Beneath the roses red and rare
She gave her life into my care,
        Gave all her heart to me;
And when beneath the mistletoe
    She standeth at my side,
    My Beautiful, my Bride,
My soul its fullest bliss shall know,
    Unheedful of the stormy tide
        On Time's mad sea.

HEAVEN'S ROSES.

I.

DEAD of night: the world is sleeping;
 Dead of winter: winds are weeping,
And a wasted form is keeping
  Vigil near her empty bed.
Here and there a coal is lying
In the gloomy grate, but dying,
  Slowly dying—all are dead.

II.

Poverina sighs! The chilly
Blast will blight the tender lily—
Ay, she sighs; her brother Willie
  May be frozen in the snow!
And she listens to the whisper
Of the weird wind, waxing crisper,
  In its monologue of woe.

III.

Willie all alone is lying
In a winding snow-shroud, dying,
And the frosty gusts are sighing
      In the bare boughs overhead ;
Willie's heart is hushed ! the whirling
Ice-wreaths round his brow are curling—
      Furling, folding o'er the dead.

IV.

Through the broken window wheeling
Snow-flakes silently are stealing,
And the orphan girl is kneeling
      Like a marble statue fair ;
And a big tear, frozen, flashes
On her closed eyes' silken lashes
      In the dip-light's fitful glare.

V.

How the storm host fiercely marches
Through the city's icy arches !
How it twirls the limes and larches
      At the rich man's, on the hill !

How its ghostly toils are stealing
O'er the gentle maiden kneeling
      At the cot-side, chill and still !

VI.

Cold the maiden grows, and colder,
As the bitter blasts enfold her,
      In the darksome dead of night ;
And a white hand stiffly closes
O'er the bosom which reposes—
Heaven is harvesting its roses—
      And her pure young soul takes flight.

FAREWELL.

I.

IS the heart I fondly fancied,
  Ah! too fondly fancied, mine,
Thus to twine its truant tendrils
  'Round another, newer shrine?
Go! The trellis from the roses
  Tear, and trail them in the dust;
Let their perfume not detain thee:
  Get thee gone—if go thou must!

II.

Dream'st thou that a heart is broken
  Like some handicraft of clay?
Think'st thou 'tis a wanton blossom
  To be plucked and thrown away?

184

Lady, go thy ways; the rustle
    Of thy garments wake a thrill
Which no coldness may extinguish,
    And a hope no fate can still.

III.

Let us strangers be forever,
    And the sea our paths divide;
Let the cold world stretch between us—
    If we be not side by side;
Let the music of thy footfall
    Never scar this heart again;
For the bliss of being near thee
    Is but servant to the pain.

IV.

Let us be unto each other
    As the palm unto the pole,
For I cast thee, as an idol,
    From the temple of my soul;
And howe'er in fond illusion
    To thy shrine my heart hath clung,
'Twas upon a cross uplifted,
    'Twas a thorn on which it hung.

V.

Then farewell! I loved thee, lady;
    Go! The roses still shall bloom
Though their tearful, tangled clusters
    Trail above Affection's tomb.
Not thy hand! 'Twere such temptation
    In its heavenly clasp to die,
That my soul had not the courage
    Nor the care to say good-by.

VI.

'Twas not mine, alas! to charm thee;
    Then how less 'tis mine to chide!
Still in wild regret I covet
    All the bliss thou hast denied;
Ah! thou canst not know the longings
    Which reflection still must wake,
Nor the smothered, choking anguish
    Of a heart too proud to break.

WHOSE IS SHE?

THEY stand in the City of Silence, hushed
    As the white stones strewed around,
And the low wind moans through the finger bones
Of the skeleton trees in its weirdest tones,
    And rustles the snow on the ground.

They crouch in the dim necropolis
    With a sinking and solemn dread,
And quake with fear that man may appear
When never a human is anywhere near,
And only the evergreen's plaint they hear
    Monotonous overhead.

Save those mute two no mortal foot
    On the ominous tryst intrudes,
And yet they descry with a fatuous eye
Full many a foe in the glooms that lie
    In the haunted solitudes.

Then silently, swiftly off and away
    Through the dim white wastes of night,
While wide flakes fall on a face and a pall,
And a form whose witchery shows through all
    Its cerements full and white.

They bear their pallid prize away,
    But out of the cedars' gloom
A sweet refrain steals again and again,
As though by reiterance still to restrain
    The ravishment of the tomb.

*   *   *   *   *

A fond mother kneels at a snow-heaped mound
    And boweth her head in prayer,
While standing above her the dead maiden's lover,
In tears, as with roses he seeketh to cover
    The ashes he dreameth are there.

And as the hot drops of their grief repeat
    Swift graves in the drifted snow,
They eagerly pray that the soul of the clay,
Adorning some star in the distance away,
To them may look down in compassion to-day
    And witness their love and their woe.

"O maiden Inona!" the lad exclaims,
　　While madly his hands entwine,
"Come back to this breast and its weary unrest—
The sun of my life hath gone down in the west—
　　Come back unto me, thou art mine!"

Then out of an old tomb standing by,
　　O'er ivied and gray, and grim,
The wind breathes low, like the fall of the snow,
"She is mine!" and the lover turns quickly to know
If man it may be making sport of his woe,
But naught can he see save an old sad tree,
　　And the tomb, and the lady by him.

Then out from the burial-yard they go,
　　But still in the wailing pine,
And in the soft dash of the snow on the sash
They listen again to the ghostly refrain,
　　　　　　　　"She is mine!"

A SIGH ON THE AIR.

I.

THERE is a sigh upon the air,
    A fading in the leaf,
And in this weary heart, a grave
    Bedewed with tears of grief.
There is a loneliness unknown
    To men I daily greet,
Which threads the desert of my soul
    With weary, friendless feet.

II.

There is a dream forever flown,
    A star in darkness set ;
There is a bitterness untold
    In all I would forget.

And from each broken bud that bends
    In Memory's acre fair,
There comes unto this weary heart
    A sigh upon the air.

III.

But faded buds shall bloom again
    When spring's soft breezes blow,
And on the grave with tears bedewed
    The violet shall grow !
What though an idle dream be flown,
    Or one fair star be set !
It may be some dim providence
    To make me happy yet.

FAITHLESS.

HOW oft my soul hath hung enchained
    Upon thy wooing tongue,
To be by brooding silence pained
    Or bitter coldness wrung!
Ah me, that in so sweet a lute
    A string should silent be!—
The golden chord, forever mute,
    That trembled once for me!

If on thy lips a queenly bloom
    From some bright Eden fell,
They caught a treacherous perfume
    From some dark source as well.
Ah me, that lips so richly fraught
    With passion's mantling morn
Could dimple to a happy thought
    While curled in cruel scorn!

If rapture rode upon thy glance
    And love thy look oppressed,
The smile but winged an angry lance
    To pierce my faithful breast.
Ah me, that eyes so fondly blue
    Could melt with tender trust,
Or with their icy lightnings strew
    Life's temples in the dust!

If on my lips the sparkling cup
    Of love hath shed its dew,
The hand which held the goblet up
    O'erturned the chalice too;
If from my life thy voice has brushed
    Some haunting cares away,
The same sweet, ruthless charm hath crushed
    Its idols into clay.

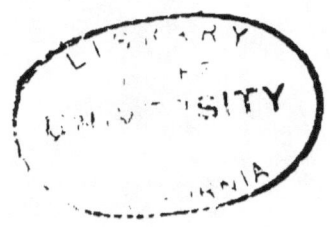